Flash Flips Out

First published in Great Britain by HarperCollins Children's Books in 2007

10 9 8 7 6 5 4 3 2 1

ISBN-10: 0-00-725307-9 ISBN-13: 978-0-00-725307-4

A CIP catalogue record for this title is available from the British Library.

The HarperCollins website address is: www.harpercollinschildrensbooks.co.uk

Based on the television series Roary the Racing Car and the original script 'Rabbit Trouble' by Wayne Jackman.

Visit Roary at: www.roarytheracingcar.com

Printed and bound in China

Flash Flips Out

HarperCollins *Children's Books*

It was another lovely day in Silver Hatch and Roary and Cici were having fun racing around the track.
But Flash was not having fun.
He was tinkering with his skateboard, way down deep in his burrow when he was rudely interrupted by a bop on the head!

Roary and Cici's super fast racing was making Flash's ceiling collapse.

"Chew my carrots!" Flash grumbled. "Those noisy race cars are driving me mad."

Back at the workshop, Mr Carburettor was looking forward to testing out his new turbo chargers on the cars.

"What's a turbo charger, Big Chris?" asked Maxi as Big Chris fitted it to his exhaust pipe.

"It's a bit of kit that will make you go faster," he explained, tightening the last nuts and bolts.

"Faster than I am already?" Maxi revved his engine, delighted. **"Fantastico!"**

"I'd better warn Flash to stay out of the way," said Molecom, disappearing into one of his tunnels.

"Are you there, Flash?" called Molecom as he popped his head up through Flash's living room floor. "You're to stay out of sight this morning so you don't mess up the test run."

"What?" Flash asked. He didn't like the sound of this at all.

"Mr Carburettor wants to know how much faster the cars can go with their new turbo chargers," Molecom explained.

"Ripen my radishes! I've got to put a stop to this" Flash cried. "It'll shake my burrow to pieces!"

Marsha was laying out safety cones on the race track when Flash spotted her with his binoculars.

"Those cones give me an idea…" he said to himself.

The cars were thrilled with their new turbo chargers.

“Wow!” said Roary. “Listen to my new engine!”

“Okay,” said Big Chris, sticking his spanner behind his ear.

“On to the starting line, you lot.”

"In a minute, Chris," Roary revved loudly. "I just want to have a practise lap first. Light 'em up!" Roary really wanted to show Mr Carburettor – and Maxi – how fast he could go.

"Roary!" yelled Big Chris as the little red car zoomed away. "Oh dear. You bend it, you mend it!"

Halfway round the racetrack, Flash was up to no good. "Hee, hee, hee," chuckled the naughty rabbit as he rearranged all of the safety cones. Soon, he had diverted the track into Farmer Green's field!

Not too far away, Roary was tearing round the track. He was just about to switch on his turbo charger when he spotted Molecom stood in the middle of the track, waving at him.

Instead of speeding up, Roary slammed on his brakes and screeched to a halt in front of his friend.

"What's the matter, Molecom?" panted Roary.

"Someone has set up the safety cones wrong, Roary!" yelped Molecom. "They take the cars right up the muddy track and into Farmer Green's yard!"

"Oh no," gasped Roary. "I'd better warn the others!" He gunned his engines and roared off to the starting line.

But Roary was too late. As he neared home, Maxi and Cici shot off from the starting grid, leaving him in a cloud of smoke. Roary spun off into a pile of tyres.

"Roary!" Big Chris yelled at the little car. "What are you playing at?"

"The safety cones are set up wrong!" Roary explained quickly. "Maxi and Cici will end up in Farmer Green's farm yard!"

"Someone must have messed around with the cones,"
Marsha said before realising who must be responsible.
"Flash!" cried Big Chris, Marsha and Mr Carburettor together.

Maxi and Cici were too far away to hear what was happening at the starting line. They were too busy rushing past one and other and trying out their turbo chargers.

Just as Cici was about to overtake Maxi, the pair spotted Flash's detour and braked hard, spinning into Farmer Green's barn and sending up clouds of smoke and dust.

Watching the race from high up in a tree, Flash chuckled to himself.

"Chew on that!" he scoffed. "They won't be bothering me for the rest of the day."

Soon, the whole gang arrived to rescue Maxi and Cici.
"Look at the state of you two!" Big Chris cried as Plugger pulled them out of the barn and back to the workshop."
A worried Mr Carburettor ran across the field.
"Maxi! Bambino! What has that Flash done to you!"
"Er, sorry everyone" Flash gulped, looking down at all the angry faces. "I was only trying to get some peace and quiet."

“Well, you certainly stopped us testing those new turbo chargers, you rascal rabbit!”
Big Chris said, sternly.

"No he didn't, Big Chris," smiled Roary cheekily. "Mine works perfectly, listen!"

And with that he revved his turbo charger loudly underneath Flash's tree. The tree rumbled and shook until Flash tumbled to the ground!

"Chew my carrots, oomph!" he grumbled, rubbing his head. Everyone laughed and Roary thought it served Flash right. Maybe he will learn that if you go around playing tricks, you sometimes come to a sticky end!

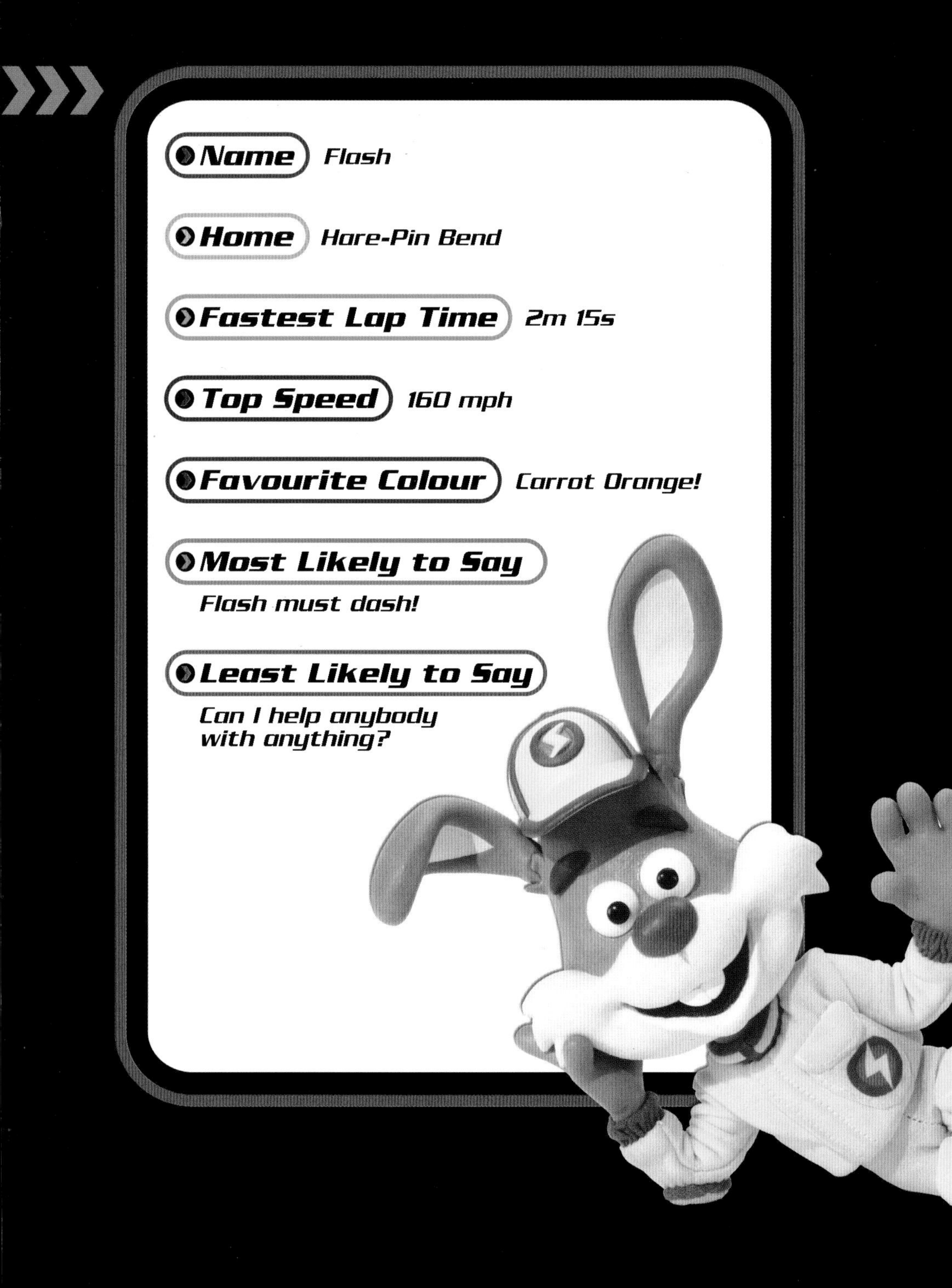

Name Flash

Home Hare-Pin Bend

Fastest Lap Time 2m 15s

Top Speed 160 mph

Favourite Colour Carrot Orange!

Most Likely to Say
Flash must dash!

Least Likely to Say
Can I help anybody
with anything?

Flash